STRIVE TO SURVIVE
YOU DECIDE WHAT HAPPENS

Trapped!

Written by
Jeanne Gowen Dennis and Sheila Seifert

Cover illustration by David Hohn
Interior illustrations by Ron Adair

www.cookcommunications.com/kidz

Faith
Building
Guide
Ages
9 and up
Worship

Faith Kidz® is an imprint of Cook Communications Ministries
Colorado Springs, Colorado 80918
Cook Communications, Paris, Ontario
Kingsway Communications, Eastbourne, England

TRAPPED!
©2003 by Jeanne Gowen Dennis and Sheila Seifert

First printing, 2003
Printed in U.S.A.
1 2 3 4 5 6 7 8 9 10 Printing/Year 07 06 05 04 03

Senior Editor: Heather Gemmen
Design Manager: Jeffrey P. Barnes
Designer: Granite Design

For my brother Timothy,
a true blessing from God. –JGD

For Riley, Molly, and Jenny Naylor. –SS

Have you ever wanted to witness the Red Sea opening or the walls of Jericho falling? The Strive to Survive series takes you into the middle of the action of your favorite Bible stories.

In each story, you are the main character. What happens is up to you! Through your choices, you can receive great rewards, get into big trouble, or even lose your life.

Your goal is to choose well and survive.
Your adventure begins now.

Trapped!

"Talmai, let's spy!" you say. Spying is your favorite game.

Your brother scowls. "I can't. I've got to watch Onan." You wrinkle your nose. Your two-year-old brother does not make a good spy, and he smells like he needs to be changed. You hurry away before Talmai asks for your help.

Once out of sight of your home, you saunter along the streets of Jericho. The sun is painting long shadows across the city.

You turn down a path that runs between Jericho's wall and the almost empty marketplace. You hear two men approaching. Undetected, you slip between cool stones into your favorite hiding place in the city wall.

"Israelite spies here? In Jericho? Are you sure?" The voice is rough. The men walk along the street near where you are hiding. They are too close for you to peek out and identify them.

"I saw them myself."

A shiver of fear creeps up your back. Real spies! You have heard that some strange, powerful people called Israelites are camped on the other side of the Jordan River. They have already defeated two mighty Amorite kings.

The men continue speaking as they move away from your hiding place. "Do you really believe that their God opened the Red Sea for them and then drowned the whole Egyptian army?"

The second man answers, "Yes, I do. Thousands of slaves couldn't possibly have defeated Pharaoh's chariots and horses. I just hope they're not planning to attack us."

"Jericho has a strong wall," says the first man. "If they dare attack, we can defeat them."

"But can we defeat their God?" asks the first.

You can no longer hear what the men are saying. You want to see the spies for yourself. You climb to a nearby roof to survey the area. You do not see anything out of the ordinary. The hay on the roof makes you sneeze.

Two men in dark robes hurry around the corner. The spies! Others are watching them like you are; only they are being more obvious. The men enter a house built into the city's wall.

Oh no! It's your Aunt Rahab's house! Aunt Rahab is your mother's sister. You like her, but

she has a way of getting into trouble. You hope that the men won't hurt her. You wonder if she could get arrested for letting foreign spies into her home.

CHOICE ONE: If you go home for supper and tell your family what you saw, go to page 9.

CHOICE TWO: If you decide to visit Aunt Rahab to find out what is going on, go to page 11.

You are hungry, and supper should be ready. So you head for home. You enter the house and shut the wooden door behind you. The scents of freshly roasted lamb and vegetables fill the room. Talmai is playing on the floor with Onan. Your baby brother looks tiny beside Talmai, who is almost as tall as your father.

"I know something you don't," you whisper to Talmai.

He ignores you. He's probably still upset that you went spying without him. Onan giggles when Talmai tickles him.

"I only hope Aunt Rahab knows what she's doing." That ought to pique his interest. You start setting your family's clay dishes on the wooden table.

Talmai says, "Come here, Onan, and I'll tickle you again."

"It's too bad," you whisper, as if talking to yourself. "But if she has to die, I hope she leaves me her house."

Talmai stops and slams his hand on the floor. "What are you talking about?"

You can't help gloating a little. "I saw some real spies today. They're from the Israelite camp by the Jordan."

Talmai says, "You watch Onan. I want to go and see the spies."

Your mother walks in with a pitcher of goat's

milk. "Help me put the food on the table, you two."

Talmai blurts out, "Aunt Rahab is in trouble, and there are spies in Jericho. Come on, Mom. Let me go."

Your mother is used to you and your brother pretending to be spies. Her voice does not change. "Maybe later. I need your help now."

Talmai complains but obeys. You go to help your mother, too.

During supper, your parents do not allow Talmai and you to talk about your spy stories, so Talmai tries to mouth questions to you. You don't understand him.

Talmai becomes frustrated and says, "I'm not going to wait until I grow up to be a soldier. I'll fight for Jericho against the Israelites now."

"I'm sure you will," says your father. "Don't talk with your mouth full."

You take a large bite of lamb to keep from laughing.

CHOICE ONE: If you describe the men for your brother after supper, go to page 91.

CHOICE TWO: If you continue teasing your brother after supper, go to page 26.

You watch Aunt Rahab's house for a while, but the men do not come out. Finally, you climb down from your hiding place and go to Aunt Rahab's door. You stare at it. Should you knock? What if the men have killed her? What will they do to you? You start to turn away, but then you change your mind. You close your eyes, grit your teeth, and knock.

Aunt Rahab calls out, "Who is it?"

"It's me, Aunt Rahab," you shout.

After a few moments, the door opens. Your aunt greets you with a smile, but before she can hug you, someone pushes past.

"We've heard reports of Israelite spies here," a soldier says. You can tell that he came from the king because of his uniform.

"We'd like to take a look around," says another soldier.

Aunt Rahab lets them in immediately. "There were some men here earlier," she tells them. "Were they really spies? I could have been killed! Oh, I'm so glad they left!"

You never saw the men leave. What is Aunt Rahab up to? Her house has only one door, and you were watching it the whole time. Your aunt is lying.

CHOICE ONE: If you do not say anything and wait for the soldiers to leave, go to page **68**.

CHOICE TWO: If you tell the men what you saw, go to page **35**.

The moment your aunt is gone, you put Onan on the floor and ask, "Can I stay with Aunt Rahab?"

"Don't be ridiculous!" your mother says. Talmai laughs at you, but you believe that what Aunt Rahab says is true. You hear a clank and spin around. It's only Onan hitting his rocks together.

That night you have a hard time sleeping. You hear every creak of your house. During breakfast the next morning, you go to the window three times, thinking you have heard something.

"Why are you so jumpy?" your father asks.

"Israel's going to attack, and if we're not at Aunt Rahab's house, we'll die," you say.

"You don't think I can protect you from them?" your father asks.

"From them, maybe," you say, "but not from their God. May I please stay with Aunt Rahab?" Your father grunts and leaves the table.

For days you startle at every noise. You are so nervous that your parents become jumpy just being around you.

One day your mother says, "Oh, let the child go." Your father rolls his eyes, but he does not stop you.

Once inside Aunt Rahab's house, you finally feel safe. Her rooms are filled with beautiful fabrics, and she smells like a wild flower. You never want to leave Aunt Rahab's house again, not even to fetch water. Talmai visits to taunt you about being such a coward.

"If Israel attacks," he says, "I'll be a brave lion, not a scared rabbit like you. Our parents are ashamed of you, and so am I." His words hurt you inside.

"Talmai, that is enough," Aunt Rahab says. "An attack is coming, and you will die if you are not with me." Once a day she leaves her home to visit with your family. "I try to convince them to stay with me, but they won't listen," she says.

If only you could think of a way to convince your family to come and be safe at Aunt Rahab's.

CHOICE ONE: If you never leave Aunt Rahab's house, go to page 77.

CHOICE TWO: If you leave to try and convince your family to go to Aunt Rahab's house, go to page 49.

"I don't know," you say, "but I want to get as far away from it as I can."

"No one is safe from magic like that," Talmai says.

"Aunt Rahab says it's their God. Let's leave now or their God might do something terrible to us for spying on them."

"We'd better go tell Mom and Dad," Talmai says. He rubs a dirty hand over his forehead as though he has a headache.

Your head hurts, too. "That's the last thing we should do," you say. "If the Israelite God is after us, we'll put our family in danger by going home."

You both start running in the opposite direction of Jericho. You eat wild berries and roots whenever you can find them and drink from streams along the way.

When you finally reach a city, the people there seem just as afraid of Israel as Talmai and you are. You wonder if you can be safe there. Should you have listened to Aunt Rahab? Talmai and you find work carrying water and supplies in the local market for several weeks.

One night, Talmai says, "I want to go home. I miss Mom and Dad."

"And Onan," you add. You both think for a while before you continue. "Israel's God hasn't done anything to us yet. Perhaps it would be okay to go home," you say. You and your brother immediately begin the journey back to Jericho.

When you reach a hill overlooking Jericho, you see only a pile of blackened rubble. You race to where the city should have been, but it isn't there. One house appears to be standing. Talmai and you climb over ruins and dead bodies to reach it. The smell of decay and ashes is everywhere. You hold your noses and try not to look.

You reach the only house that is still standing. The door has been burnt off and the inside has been gutted by fire. Sunlight is shining through the window and you see something hanging outside. It has been singed, but you recognize it as Aunt Rahab's red cord.

"It's Aunt Rahab's house!" you shout. "See the cord?"

Talmai nods and then shakes his head. "I wonder if she made it out of Jericho okay."

"I wonder if our family was with her," you say.

You leave Jericho, because there is nothing left for you there. You do not even look back. It is too painful.

"Aunt Rahab must be with the Israelites," you say. "Maybe if we go to them they will have mercy on us and let us stay with her."

"Aren't you afraid of what their God will do to us?"

"I am more afraid of never knowing the truth. I want to find out if Aunt Rahab and maybe even our parents and Onan are alive." You head in the direction of the Israelite camp.

When you reach it, you are overjoyed to see your aunt alive. You and Talmai give her an enormous hug, but neither one of you can ask the question on your mind.

"I know it's only been a couple of weeks, but I think you've both grown," she says. Her eyes are moist as if she is about to cry, but she blinks the tears back. "Where have you been?"

You and Talmai tell her of your adventures. Then you stop and look to the ground. You are so afraid of finding out that your family did not survive.

Finally, Talmai asks, "Are our parents and Onan here?"

Aunt Rahab bites her bottom lip, and then says, "When you two disappeared, your father searched everywhere for you. He was a broken man. He was so distressed that he began to listen to what I said about Israel's God. He even got your mother to listen. When Israel attacked, your whole family was in my house. They are all safe."

You smile. Your heart feels light. Just then, you see your father in the distance. He's holding Onan. You and Talmai run to him and are engulfed in an enormous bear hug. If your father has chosen to believe in Israel's God, then you are going to believe in him also.

THE END

You believe the rumors. Israel has been marching around the city one time each day for about a week. They are marching longer than normal this morning. Something must be up. Talmai and your father prepare to fight. You, your mother, and Onan run to your safest hiding place in Jericho's wall. You have put blankets, food, water, and extra clothing there. Now all you have to do is wait—and keep Onan quiet if the enemy gets near.

The sounds outside of your hiding place are dulled, because you are in the middle of the thickest part of the wall. Then you hear a sound as if the earth's stomach were growling. That sound is loud and is not muffled at all. Onan begins to cry. You feel like crying, too. Your mother screams.

Without warning, Jericho's wall starts to shake. Your hiding place crumbles. The wall that you thought would protect you kills you and your family.

THE END

Since Onan likes going to the inn, and people from all over hang around it, you decide to go there. You stoop down to Onan's level and say, "Want to go to the inn? Want to see Father?"

Onan squeals with delight. He starts toddling toward the door. You pull him into your arms, laughing.

The streets are crowded with merchants selling their wares. Pigs, sheep, and goats wait in stalls for purchase, filling the air with grunting and bleating, as well as some odors you would rather not smell. You hurry past.

When you reach the inn, you set Onan in a chair with some dates to eat. He plays with them and gets his hands, face, and hair sticky.

While you are cleaning him, you hear a soldier say, "Israel has sent spies into Jericho."

"I heard that they escaped, so the king's men went after them," says a merchant.

"I hope you're right," says the soldier. "Those Israelites have some unbelievable power behind them."

A third man's voice cracks as he tells about the power of Israel's God. When you look up, you are surprised to see that most of the men look a little nervous. Some are even trembling! You catch your father's eye.

"Don't worry," your father says. "Jericho's wall will protect us."

"You aren't afraid then?" You move your weight from one foot to another.

"No, and you shouldn't be either. Now take this little boy home for his nap."

You wish you could be like your father. You know that Jericho's soldiers are strong and fierce. You have watched them fight from the safety of your hiding places. But you are afraid. You look at your little brother falling asleep sitting up. He is so cute. What if someone should hurt him?

CHOICE ONE: If you go home and talk to Talmai about what you heard, go to page 56.

CHOICE TWO: If you run away to protect your baby brother, go to page 30.

You leave for another city. The journey is long and hard. Onan sometimes walks and sometimes has to be carried. You do not know which is worse. When he walks, he stops to look at rocks, bugs, or plants every few feet. When you carry him, your arms and back ache.

After several days of walking, you have not come to a city. You should have been there by now. With a sinking heart, you realize that you are lost—and you have run out of food. You sit down and cry. Onan climbs on your lap, pats your face, and tries to make you feel better. You hug him.

"You feel better now?" he asks.

You do not want to disappoint him, so you say, "Yes, I feel better."

He hops off your lap. "Okay, we go play."

Moping around will not help, so you get up and chase Onan around some bushes. His giggles make everything seem okay again. You grab him and spin him around. "I love you, Onan," you say.

"I wuv you, too," he shouts between giggles. You set him down on the ground and support him while he regains his balance.

"I'm hungry," he says. Suddenly he points and squeals. "Horses!" Onan loves animals, but he sometimes gets mixed up on their names. You look behind you to see what's really there. Camels! It appears to be a caravan, and they are coming right toward you.

Could they be friendly? Surely they would not hurt two lost and starving children. You walk toward them. When you meet, the leader greets you. You tell him that you are lost. They are from a far-off country, and they offer to take you home with them.

"Are there any Israelites in your country?" you ask.

"What is an Israelite?" the leader asks.

"It doesn't matter," you say with a smile. You do not like leaving your home, but at least with this man you believe you and Onan will be safe. You offer yourself as his servant if he will help you take care of your brother.

You go to the man's home and serve his kind family for many years.

THE END

You start yelling and waving your arms, trying to convince your parents to go to Aunt Rahab's house. Talmai joins in.

"It's true! Every word. If you don't believe us, you won't go to Aunt Rahab's house, and we're all going to die!"

Your mother feels your foreheads. "You've both had too much sun today. Here, drink some water, and then I want you both to lie down."

"They're acting crazy," says your father as he leaves the room.

Finally, after days of pleading, they allow you both to go stay with Aunt Rahab. From her window, you watch the forces of Israel march around the city wall, but afterwards they leave. Aunt Rahab is certain the attack will come soon. You watch the army repeat this day after day. Talmai and you play games on the floor or help Aunt Rahab feed your relatives. Many have come to her house for safety. Talmai and you are worried about little Onan and your parents, who have not come. Finally, you work together to devise a plan.

After everyone is asleep, Talmai and you sneak out into the street. Silently, you work your way across town to your house. You climb through a window. Baby Onan is asleep on a mat. Talmai wraps him in a blanket and carries him to the window while you leave a note for your parents to come to Aunt Rahab's house. You are glad that your father taught you to write.

Your note says, "Onan is with us. Please come to Aunt Rahab's so we will all be safe together."

You climb out the window, and Talmai hands Onan to you. He stirs a little, but you rock him in your arms to get him back to sleep. He feels much heavier when he's asleep. You take turns carrying him to Aunt Rahab's house.

In the morning, your parents come to Aunt Rahab's, but only to get Onan. They have no intention of staying.

"The least you can do is look out the window at the Israelites," Rahab says to try to convince them to stay. Out of curiosity, they do look out the window to see the soldiers, and they welcome some of the food Aunt Rahab has prepared with your help.

Finally, they get up to leave. Talmai and you have already planned for this. While they were not looking, you slowly piled rocks, furniture, bedding, and even some flax stalks from the roof against the door. You sit on top of them and refuse to move. Your father is angry.

Just as he is about to thrash you for your stubbornness, you hear a piercing note from the trumpets and loud shouting. You feel the earth shaking around you. The wall of Jericho has fallen, but your family is safe!

THE END

After dinner, Talmai and you go outside. Talmai asks, "Who are these spies? What do they look like?"

You say, "I must be one of the most important people in town since I spotted the foreigners. Maybe the king will give me a reward of shiny gold coins if I tell him what I saw."

"What did you see?" Talmai demands. "Is Jericho in danger?"

"Could be. I'd give up the idea of fighting, though. Relatives of traitors might not be allowed in the army."

"What are you talking about?"

You lean over the wall of the well and smell the moist stones. "Wouldn't you like to know." You hurry past him toward your father's inn. Talmai follows.

He grabs your arm. "Tell me what's going on!"

You kick him to try and get away. Even though you pull and twist, he does not let go. Your hand is going numb. Just as you are about to give up and tell him what he wants to know, you see your father. You let out your most painful-sounding moan.

Just as you hoped, your father comes over and pulls you apart.

"Stop it, both of you!" He is about to leave.

Talmai's eyes narrow. You have pushed him

too far. You do not want to be alone with him. You begin to cry loudly.

"That's enough!" your father says. "Go home. Go to bed at once. Both of you. And I don't want to hear another sound from either of you!"

You run home before Talmai can take out his anger on you. You lie down on your mat and turn your face to the wall. Talmai arrives after you. Without a word, he moves his mat away from yours and falls heavily onto it. The room grows dark.

You begin to regret picking a fight with your brother. You try to whisper to him, but he has either fallen asleep or is refusing to talk to you. You decide to make it up to him in the morning by telling him everything.

When the sun rises, Talmai is gone, and so is your father's sword. You never see him again. One day, you hear a rumor that he was killed trying to fight the Israelites all alone.

You blame yourself. You are so upset that you ignore everything that is happening around you. Even the lamb that you normally love so well tastes bland. Each day is a blur to you, until the day Israel attacks. The wall falls with a crash, and there is a cloud of dust in the air that makes it hard to breathe. You see a soldier coming at you with a sword. It is then that you come alive again. You want to avenge your brother's death. You grab a knife and a sharp stick and go toward him. You fight bravely, but you are no match for a grown-up warrior. You die in battle.

THE END

You hold still until the men disappear into the blackness of the Jericho plain. Just then, a guard comes by on his nightly rounds.

"You there!" You can see by the shadow of his bow and arrow that he is ready to shoot.

"Don't shoot! I'm a child of Jericho," you shout.

He lowers the bow and walks over to you. "Don't you know better than to play up here after dark? I could have mistaken you for a spy. Now go home."

The soldier means business. You climb down as fast as you can.

"Don't let me catch you up here after dark again," he says.

You reach the street, panting. That was close.

CHOICE ONE: If you go to Aunt Rahab's to ask her about the strangers, go to page 60.

CHOICE TWO: If you go home and tell your brother what you saw, go to page 48.

You decide to try to protect your baby brother by running away. While he is taking his nap at home, you gather up food, clothing, and other supplies. You leave a note for your family and then sneak out carrying the sleeping Onan.

When you reach the city gate, it is crowded with people. The adults are so busy arguing about Israel that no one notices you leaving. You make your way across the plain and hide in the hills nearby. One time you think you see two men who look like foreigners, but they quickly disappear. Could they be the spies who visited Aunt Rahab? If they are, then the king's men were looking for them in the wrong direction!

You play with your brother by day, and sleep beside him at night. You have found a cave for your home. Each day, you go to a place where you can see Jericho and watch what is happening. It is funny, but no one seems to be coming or going. The gate never opens.

One day you see people marching from the plain to Jericho. It must be the Israelites! They are blowing horns of some kind. You can hear them faintly, but you can't quite see them. The army marches all the way around the wall that surrounds Jericho. Then they leave. You wonder what they are doing.

For the next three days, the same thing happens. You are not sure what to do, but watching

Onan in the hills is getting harder and harder. Yesterday he was almost bitten by a snake, and you are beginning to run out of food. As you chew on a hard piece of bread that tastes more like your sandals than your mother's cooking, you decide to go home. The Israelites are probably not as bad as you imagined.

You wait until Onan is asleep. Then you pick him up and make your way back to Jericho's gate. It is locked! Try as you might, you can't get in. You have to go somewhere else, but where?

CHOICE ONE: If you leave for another city, go to page 22.

CHOICE TWO: If you go back to the hills and wait for the gate to open, go to page 69.

"Talmai sleeping?" Onan asks.

You shake Talmai, but he is still unconscious. "Come on, wake up," you say. "Onan, help me wake up Talmai."

Onan climbs on top of Talmai's stomach repeating, "Wake up! Wake up!" He tries to stand up and then plops his whole weight on Talmai's stomach.

Talmai groans. You help him sit up. His head is bleeding a little.

"Come on," you say to Talmai, "We have to get someone to fix that cut. Aunt Rahab's house is closest."

Talmai is too dazed to argue. You support him with one arm and carry Onan with the other. You feel like your arms are breaking by the time you reach Aunt Rahab's house. She was watching for you.

"Quick," she says, "get inside." There is blood everywhere, and Talmai looks really pale. It scares you a little.

"Shouldn't we get Mother and Father here to see to Talmai?" you ask as one of your other aunts cleans the wound.

Aunt Rahab opens her door and calls to a merchant across the street. "Abi, could your servant run and find my sister right away? Her son has been hurt. He's bleeding."

"Of course," Abi calls back.

"Please hurry! Please," Aunt Rahab says. The urgency in her voice makes you wonder. Talmai is hurt, but his wound is not life-threatening. Could her urgency have something to do with the Israelites marching outside?

You want to look out the window, but you will not leave Talmai's side. You feel responsible for his injury, and you want him to know how sorry you are. Most of the family are crowded at the window, leaning out to see what is happening below.

Your cousin says, "This is the fourth time that they are marching around." By the time your parents come through the door, your cousin says, "That makes the seventh time."

"Talmai, are you okay?" your mother asks. A loud shout from outside drowns her next words. Almost immediately, there is a creaking and groaning, as if the very earth beneath you is moving. It becomes a rumble, like a thunderstorm, that shakes the house. Talmai holds onto you and your mother. Your father picks up Onan, and you huddle together. Everything shakes. A clay pot falls off one of Aunt Rahab's shelves and crashes to the floor. The room fills with a cloud of dirt and covers each of you. It makes your eyes water and tastes like dry mud pies. Onan begins to cry, choking on the air as he gasps for breath.

You focus your eyes on the red cord hanging from the window, the sign to the Israelites that Aunt

Rahab's family is inside. You hear yelling men and the screams of women along with the clanking of metal. Then suddenly Aunt Rahab's door bursts open, and Israelite soldiers stand in the doorway. Their faces are fierce looking and their weapons have blood on them.

"Rahab?" says the soldier in front. His voice is not as rough as he looks.

Aunt Rahab nods. "I am Rahab. These are my relatives."

"Come with me," he says, "all of you. We'll get you out of here safely." You give a sigh of relief. You did not know that you had been holding your breath. You are alive! Your whole family is safe! From deep inside your heart, you give thanks to Israel's God. When you get out of here, you want to learn more about him.

THE END

Aunt Rahab's lie could be putting the whole city in danger.

"I saw the men, too," you say. "And they never—"

"Silence!" demands one of the soldiers. He pushes you aside. "We didn't ask you."

Aunt Rahab continues her story. "The men left at dusk, when the city gates were closing. If you hurry, you may be able to catch them." The men thank her and leave. "Go quickly!" she calls after them.

When the door is shut behind them, you look at your aunt suspiciously.

She smiles. "Sit down, dear. I have something to tell you."

You look around the room, wondering where the men are hiding.

Aunt Rahab says, "Jericho is in great danger. Even if we fight against Israel, we will not win."

Her words frighten you. You look at the door, wanting to run out of it.

CHOICE ONE: If you stay and ask your aunt to explain, go to page 86.

CHOICE TWO: If you run out of the house, refusing to hear any more, go to page 52.

You carry Onan to Aunt Rahab's house and knock. She does not answer the door. She must not be home. You wander around the city for a while and show Onan the market stalls on the way home. The merchants are selling everything you can imagine—silk, salt, and fruits that do not grow around Jericho. You wonder if someday you would like to be a merchant.

When you arrive home, you find that Aunt Rahab is there, with your mother. They are yelling at each other.

Your mother says, "I refuse to listen to any more of your nonsense."

You lay Onan down for his nap. Then Talmai and you go outside. "What's going on in there?" you ask.

"Aunt Rahab wants us all to stay with her if Israel attacks. She says that that's the only way we'll be safe. Mother thinks she's crazy."

"What do you think?"

"I'm not sure. Some of what Aunt Rahab says makes sense. I want to find out more about it."

Aunt Rahab comes out. "Please, children. Come to my house when Israel attacks and try to get your mother and father there, too." She leaves.

Later, you ask your mother, "What were you fighting with Aunt Rahab about? Was she being mean to you?"

Your mother laughs, but her face is angry.

"She wasn't being mean to me but to all of Jericho. She helped Israelite spies!"

You shake your head. "Israel is our enemy." Still, you do not like it when your mother and Aunt Rahab are upset with each other.

Soon the gates of Jericho are closed, and no one is allowed in or out. You feel trapped. Now only soldiers are allowed on the top of the wall. That is where all your favorite spying spots are. Aunt Rahab's window provides a great view of the outside. But you do not want your mother to feel that you are siding with Aunt Rahab against her.

CHOICE ONE: If you stay away from Aunt Rahab's house, go to page 63.

CHOICE TWO: If you visit Aunt Rahab, go to page 82.

You shake your head. "She let foreign spies enter her home. How can we believe what she says?"

Talmai adds, "Maybe she even helped them to escape."

The thought that Aunt Rahab might have helped Jericho's enemy eats away at you for days. When you can't take it anymore, you ask Talmai, "Do you want to sneak out of Jericho with me and spy on the foreigners?"

"We'll leave as soon as the gates open tomorrow," Talmai says.

The next morning, the weather is perfect for spying. You pass through the city gate as if you have no more on your mind than catching dinner.

"Hello," you call to the two gatekeepers. "It looks like good weather for fishing at the Jordan River today."

"Watch out for foreigners," one of them warns.

"We will." You wave to thank him for his advice and move on. Your heart is beating violently with excitement, so you make yourself take deep, slow breaths.

Finally, you are out of the city. You love the smell of the wild grasses around Jericho. You break off an especially long weed and stick it between your teeth.

"I'll race you to the river," Talmai says, hitting

the end of the weed and sprinting away from you.

It is too far to run the entire way. When you both get tired, you walk side by side. By mid-morning you have found the area across the river from where the Israelites are camping. Talmai finds a great hiding place behind some bushes. You join him. The Israelites appear to be packing.

"Maybe they're going back the way they came," you say. "They certainly can't get all those people and supplies across the river. Look how the water is swelling up. It's practically ready to flood over the banks."

As if on cue, the wind changes and blows wildly in your direction. The roar of the water almost drowns out Talmai's voice. "What do you think that box is? Do you see it?"

You scan the opposite bank. At first, you see only hundreds of people milling around. Then you notice some men carrying a large box on poles. It looks like it is made out of gold with wings on the top of it. It takes four men in fancy clothes to carry it. The men walk as if they are performing some type of ritual. They slowly make their way to the river. Suddenly, a deafening roar and a strong wind make both Talmai and you close your eyes and duck.

"Aaaahhh!" Talmai and you scream.

By the time you look up, you can't speak. The river upstream has stopped flowing.

Downstream, the water has all run off. There is no river at all!

The robed men have carried the strange box with poles into the riverbed. You expect them to sink or at least slip on the muddy bottom, but they are walking on dry land! All the Israelite soldiers and their families start crossing the Jordan as if there had never been a river there.

"Let's get out of here!" Talmai says.

You both take off running. Talmai is ahead of you. As you try to catch up, your heart is beating so hard that you can hardly breathe. You run until you can no longer see where the river used to be. Finally, you both stop to rest.

"What was that box?" Talmai asks. "What kind of magic did they use?" The heat from the sun is beating down on you, but you are shivering with fear.

You try to answer between pants. "I don't know. But now I'm sure that Aunt Rahab was telling the truth." Your side aches.

"What should we do?" Talmai asks.

CHOICE ONE: If you run as far away as you can, go to page 15.

CHOICE TWO: If you go back to Jericho to warn your family, go to page 75.

You move closer to the edge of the wall so you can see a little better. The man has reached the ground. Holding onto the wall, you lean over further to see his face in the moonlight. A section of the wall comes loose, and your hand slips. You try to catch yourself, but you leaned over too far. As you tumble over the edge, you remember hearing that people see their whole life passing before their eyes before they die. Twelve years goes by really fast.

THE END

You ignore Talmai, pick up Onan, and run to Aunt Rahab's house. You are glad that Talmai does not follow you. Instead of playing, you sit and think. Today's incident with Talmai scared you. Your family is putting Onan's life at risk. Before your mother comes to take him home, you hide him in one of your secret hiding places in the wall. It's not far from Aunt Rahab's, so you can get him to safety quickly.

"I'll come back for you in just a little while," you tell him. He's sleepy, so you cover him with a blanket and give him a toy made of lamb's wool to hold. He falls asleep.

When your mother comes to get Onan, you tell her that he is hidden, and you will not tell anyone where he is unless the whole family comes to Aunt Rahab's.

"Israel has been marching around this city every day," you say. "One of these days, they're not just going to march. They're going to attack. I can't let Onan die." Your mother is upset and worried about Onan. Aunt Rahab and the other relatives finally convince her to come stay with you.

"After all," Aunt Rahab says, "If they don't attack, what could it hurt? We'll just have a family reunion. If they do attack, then you will all be safe with us."

Your mother promises to come the next day. You assure her that Onan will be safe with you. As soon as she leaves, you go get your brother. He snuggles into your arms. You are grateful that your plan worked, and that he will be safe.

The next morning, Israel's soldiers change their routine. You feel sure the attack is coming. The rest of your family has not yet made it to Aunt Rahab's.

CHOICE ONE: If you wait at Aunt Rahab's for them to come, go to page 47.

CHOICE TWO: If you run home to get your family, go to page 84.

You calm down, take a deep breath, and tell your story again, including every detail you can remember. Your mother's eyes soften a little, but your father becomes stern.

"Enough of your spy stories," he tells you. "Get to your chores." Talmai and you go outside to thresh some barley.

As you beat the stalks to release the grains, Talmai asks, "Why won't they believe us?"

"If you think about it, why would they believe us? We watched something that should have been impossible. And we have told some whopping spy stories before."

"I guess you're right. All we can do is keep telling them the truth until they believe us."

You think Talmai's idea is a good one. Every day, you both tell your parents about your frightening experience at the Jordan River. Rumors that support your story are spreading around the city. Finally, your parents believe you.

Then one day, the Israelites show up outside the city wall. Immediately, your father sends you, your brothers, and your mother to Aunt Rahab's house.

"Aren't you coming?" you ask.

"I have to take care of the inn," he says.

At your aunt's house, Talmai and you watch the Israelites from the window in the wall. They do not try to attack. They do not even look like they want to attack. They just march around the city. Then they leave.

"What was that for?" Talmai asks.

You shrug. Soon you all head for home.

The next day, the same thing happens. And then again a third day and a fourth day. Tomorrow will be the fifth day. The Israelites must be planning to attack soon. Each morning, you have begged your father to come with you, but he says he needs to take care of his customers at the inn. Since your father will not listen to you, you decide to try a different tactic.

CHOICE ONE: If you go to the inn with your father, go to page 88.

CHOICE TWO: If you try to force him to go to Aunt Rahab's, go to page 73.

You wait for your family to come, just as your mother promised. Over and over, you watch out the window to see what Israel is doing and then run to the door to watch for your family. Finally, when Israel has almost marched around the city for the seventh time, your parents arrive.

"Where's Talmai?" you ask, with terror in your heart.

"He refused to come," says your mother. "Maybe he'll change his mind later."

But it is too late. The walls come crashing down around you. Only those in Aunt Rahab's house survive.

THE END

You run home. After supper, you pull your brother Talmai aside and whisper, "Listen." You tell him about what you saw.

He says, "I've heard people talking today about Israel. They defeated two powerful Amorite kings on the other side of the Jordan River.

That scares you. "Do you think they'll come here?"

"Let them come," he says. Talmai is bigger and stronger than you are. Perhaps it is easier to be brave when one is not so small. He continues, "They can't possibly get through our city wall, but if they do, we'll beat them. I'm ready to fight."

You nod, but you are still a little scared. The next day, it is your turn to watch Onan. You think about taking him either to the inn or to see Aunt Rahab. You want to talk to someone about what you saw or at least gather more information.

CHOICE ONE: If you go to the inn, go to page 20.

CHOICE TWO: If you go see Aunt Rahab, go to page 36.

Out on the plains, you can see Israel's camp-site. You know they will attack soon. Your heart aches to think that harm will come to your family. You keep reminding yourself of how much you love your family as you open the door, step outside, and walk away from Aunt Rahab's house.

When you reach home, your father says, "Who is this stranger?" Your mother's hug is so tight and long that you wonder if she will ever let you go. You don't mind, really. You have missed her and the good smells of her cooking that are deep within everything. Even Talmai's punch on your arm and Onan's slobbering kiss welcome you.

"Please come back to Aunt Rahab's with me," you say. "Israel has crossed the Jordan and is camped just beyond Jericho."

Your father says, "Jericho's wall has been built and rebuilt over hundreds of years. It is so strong and thick now, that no army can breach it. Stop worrying so much and come home."

"Yes, stay and help," says Talmai. "I'm sick of doing your chores and mine, too."

His words give you an idea. "I'm going back to Aunt Rahab's, but I can take Onan with me. I can take care of him there. That will help, won't it?"

"That would lessen Talmai's load," your mother says. "You can come get Onan in the morning, and then I'll bring him home each evening.

"I'll watch Onan," Talmai says. "Watching him

is easy compared to the other chores." You wonder
if big strong Talmai really means that or if he's
going to miss Onan.

You say, "Onan can stay with me day and
night."

Your mother shakes her head. "During the
day is enough."

"That's not fair." Talmai pouts when no one
pays him any attention.

You carry Onan's things in a sack and take
him to Aunt Rahab's house. He wants to get down
and walk partway. You watch him toddle on his
chubby legs, and you are glad that he will be at the
house with you. Every few feet, he stops to pick up
a stone or to peek through a doorway. It's funny
how a simple walk can be such a great adventure
to a two-year-old.

When you reach Aunt Rahab's house, you
feel a little less afraid. Aunt Rahab is delighted to
have Onan around. Each evening your mother
comes to get him. Sometimes she stays to talk with
her sister and the other relatives who are staying
there. Each morning, you run home and bring Onan
back.

Whenever you do, Talmai says, "Don't take
him. It's not fair the way you have split up our family. Onan is my brother, too. I'll watch him." You
are surprised at how soft your brother's heart has
become.

One day, he follows after you, trying to get Onan back. You hear Israel's trumpets in the distance and know that they are already marching around the city. You have a feeling that the attack will come soon.

CHOICE ONE: If you pick up Onan and run to Aunt Rahab's house, go to page 43.

CHOICE TWO: If you try to convince Talmai to go with you, go to page 58.

The more you think about the spies, the more scared you become.

"I have to go," you say.

"Wait," she pleads. You ignore her words and race down the darkening streets, weaving your way through empty market stalls. You are looking back when someone blocks your path. You practically bounce off his protruding belly.

"Uncle Bela!" You give him an enormous hug. Your father's brother is your favorite uncle. "I'm sorry I ran into you. I didn't see you there." He is a traveling merchant and only comes to Jericho twice a year. "When did you get here?" you ask.

"Oh, I've been here a few days. Been meaning to get over to see your family. No time now, though."

"Why not?"

"I've been hearing rumors, and I don't like them one bit. Those Israelites—have you heard of them?"

"Yes, I think they sent some spies here."

"Well, that does it for me. I'm getting out of town tomorrow."

You do not know what makes you say it, but you ask, "Can I go with you? I want to get out of Jericho, too."

Your uncle rubs his chin. He always does that when he is thinking. "Why not? In fact, I think your whole family should come with me. I've been meaning to talk to your father about a business idea. His inn is doing pretty well here, but I believe that he would do much better in my town. With my goods and his know-how, we could be a great success."

Your uncle goes home with you. He and your father talk well into the night. Finally, it is decided. You will all go with your uncle. You take all your possessions with you. It takes seven days to reach your uncle's town.

At first, the new city is strange to you. You learn to like it after being there only two full moons. Every day you help your father at his new inn. Travelers coming to the inn talk about all the cities Israel has defeated, including Jericho. When you overhear their conversations, you wonder what happened to Aunt Rahab. You hope your new city will not be the next to fall.

THE END

When you really think about what your aunt said, it makes sense. Gods of wood and stone are not gods at all. You decide to trust Aunt Rahab.

On your way home, you round the corner where you first saw the strangers. Was it only a coincidence that you spotted them? Maybe there was a reason. Tomorrow you will try to find out more about the Israelites and their God.

The next day, you help your father at the inn. You listen carefully to what his customers are saying.

One man says, "The Israelite God has magical powers to open up the sea."

You ask your father, "What does that man mean?"

"It was years ago at the Red Sea," he says. "The Israelites used to be slaves in Egypt. Pharaoh's army was chasing after them and supposedly the sea opened up for the Israelites. Then it closed in over Pharaoh's army. I'm not sure I believe it, though. Here, serve this at table six."

You take two earthenware platters of meat and vegetables to a table near the door.

One man is talking to his companions at the table. "I've never heard of a god who can open up seas and help a bunch of slaves defeat powerful armies."

"It's true," another says. "And they defeated not one, but two Amorite kings, Sihon and Og." By his dusty clothes you can tell he has been traveling.

"Two?" The man whistles. "They must have learned soldiering from the Egyptians."

"No, it's just this God of theirs. The power they have is like nothing I've ever seen before. How can we begin to fight such a force?"

"Maybe we can find their god and steal it from them. Then we could have the power."

"That's just it. No one has even seen their God. It's as though he's alive and invisible. This whole business scares me. I'm getting as far away from here as I can, and I'd advise you to do the same."

All the talk frightens you. When your father is looking the other way, you slip out and start running as fast as you can. When you stop for breath, you are near the city wall. If you turn to the right, the road will take you to Aunt Rahab's house. If you turn left, it will take you to the city gate.

CHOICE ONE: If you turn right, go to page 70.

CHOICE TWO: If you turn left, go to page 78.

You go home, put Onan to bed with a kiss, and find Talmai. You tell him about what you heard.

"I'm scared of Israel's God," you say. You grab a fig from the table and pop the sweet, gritty fruit into your mouth. You chew it quickly.

Talmai waves a hand at you. "I don't know why you and Jericho's soldiers are scared. You're all a bunch of cowards!"

"But Talmai, men can't fight the gods," you say.

"I'm ashamed of you and them," he says. "Jericho needs soldiers who will stand up to their enemies without fear. I am not afraid to fight."

You feel ashamed for your cowardice. Talmai makes plans to practice with your father's sword every day. You decide to ignore your fears and do something about the upcoming battle. You search all of Jericho for the best hiding places. When the time comes, you will be able to keep Onan safe.

Aunt Rahab comes over to talk to your family about the spies. "Come to my house, please." Your father and brother leave the room, and your mother shakes her head no. Even you do not look her in the eyes.

Then one day, you hear rumors that Israel is going to attack.

CHOICE ONE: If you believe the rumors, go to page **18.**

CHOICE TWO: If you don't believe the rumors, go to page **90.**

You turn to Talmai with Onan in your arms. "Why should Onan die because you are so stubborn? Jericho doesn't have a chance against Israel."

"How can you say that? All they do is march around. They're too scared to even attack." Talmai looms over you. You know that if he wanted, he could force Onan from your arms.

"Israel does not seem to be the fierce army I expected, but their God is strong. Aunt Rahab has told me that their God is the one we should fear." You lean against a building and feel the coolness of the stones on your back. From a nearby house, you smell the scent of someone cooking sweet berries, just as if it were a normal day.

"You're a traitor!" Talmai whispers. "You're a traitor to our city and our gods. What if the king hears you? His soldiers will kill you and Onan, too. I won't let you take him." He snatches Onan from you.

Before he can leave, you grab onto Talmai's arm and hold it with all your strength so that he cannot leave with Onan. Onan starts crying.

Talmai tries to comfort him. "It's okay, little one." His arms loosen. You see your chance. You grab Onan. Talmai staggers backwards off-balance. He falls with a thunk! His head hits a stone wall.

CHOICE ONE: If you take Onan safely to Aunt Rahab's and then return to help Talmai, go to page 65.

CHOICE TWO: If you try to wake up Talmai from uncon- sciousness, go to page 32.

You give in to your curiosity and decide to go to Aunt Rahab's house. "It's me again, Aunt Rahab," you call as you knock. She lets you in immediately.

She seems happy to see you. "What brings you back so soon?"

You pull her away from the door, just in case someone walks by. "I was just on top of the wall and saw the men climb down from your window. What's going on?"

"I couldn't say anything earlier, but they were Israelites."

"And you let them go? Why?" you ask.

Your aunt sits you down and pulls a chair close to yours. "I did it to save our family. Israel will defeat Jericho."

This statement makes you angry. You stand up and face her. One of her soft pillows falls to the floor.

"Jericho is strong! Just look at the wall out there. Your own house is built on it."

Aunt Rahab rests her hands on your arms.

"Listen to me," she says. "Every man in Jericho is trembling with fear because of these Israelites and their God."

"My father isn't afraid. He says they were just rumors and that our gods will protect us." You wish your father were here right now, holding his strong arms around you.

She holds your hands in hers. "What are

Jericho's gods made of?"

You have to think about it. "Stone, wood, and stuff like that."

"Where did they come from?"

"The carvers made them. You know that." You wonder where she is going with this conversation. Everyone in Jericho knows the old man who chips away at wood and his brother who carves stones into the shapes of the gods.

"So you believe that these gods carved by men and made of stone and wood can save you?"

When you think of it that way, it does not make any sense.

She continues. "Israel's God is a living God, more powerful than we can imagine. I believe in their God." You should not have been surprised. Aunt Rahab has always been a little different.

Aunt Rahab continues. "The spies promised they would keep our family safe when their God gives Israel the land. But everyone has to be inside my house, or they will die."

You are not sure what to believe. Why should you or your aunt trust what the Israelites said? Were they just lying to save themselves? Or were they telling the truth?

CHOICE ONE: If you decide that your aunt was fooled, go to page 79.

CHOICE TWO: If you decide to trust your aunt's judgment, go to page 54.

You decide to stay away from Aunt Rahab's house to please your mother, but you are curious to find out more about the Israelite spies. Since Talmai runs errands for your father for the next couple of weeks, you ask him to visit Aunt Rahab and find out all he can. In that way, he can tell you what he finds out. You stay home and help your mother.

After a few days, you see a difference in Talmai. He does not seem as ready to fight as before.

"What would it hurt to go to her house?" he asks. "We can fight there just as easily as anywhere else. And if what Aunt Rahab says is true, then we'll be safe."

What Talmai says makes sense. You both start working on your parents to get them to agree to go to Aunt Rahab's house.

Your mother says, "I'll think about it." Your father will not even consider it.

One day when you are working outside and watching Onan, Talmai comes running. "Come quickly, before it's too late!"

"Is it the attack?" you ask.

"Yes, hurry!" he says. Both of your parents are at the inn. You hurry there and try to get them to come with you.

"You go ahead," your mother says. "I'll come a little later."

"An attack?" your father says sarcastically.

"What a bunch of nonsense."

You, Talmai, and Onan are in Aunt Rahab's house when the wall falls down. After the attack, you are orphans. You and your brothers live with Aunt Rahab and the Israelites. Talmai is the first to believe in Israel's God. At first, you do not want to believe, because you are angry about your parents' deaths.

"They had a chance to be saved," Talmai reminds you. "It was their choice not to go to Aunt Rahab's house."

Finally, you believe in the living God, too, and Talmai and you talk to Onan about him every day.

THE END

You take off your cloak and cover Talmai with it. Then you race to Aunt Rahab's house.

You tell her, "Talmai tried to take Onan from me. Then he fell back and hurt his head." You give Onan a big hug and leave him with your aunt. Then you rush back to where you left Talmai. He is still unconscious.

You try shaking him as you call, "Talmai. Talmai! Talmai wake up!" He still does not revive.

You roll him onto your cloak. His head is bleeding a little. You pull on the cloak to drag Talmai along the street. When you go over a big bump, Talmai wakes up.

"What happened?" he asks.

"You hit your head. It's bleeding, and we have to get someone to bandage it." You help him struggle to his feet.

Suddenly, he remembers. "Where's Onan? We've lost Onan!"

"Calm down," you say. "He's safe at Aunt Rahab's. You'll see him in a few minutes."

Talmai stands and takes a step. He is moving very slowly.

"I'm dizzy," he says. "I want to stop and rest, maybe take a nap in the shade."

"No!" you say. "You hit your head hard. You have to stay awake until Aunt Rahab looks at you."

Step by step, you get closer to the house. You can hear the trumpets and the marching outside, and your heart beats faster. You have to reach the door in time!

The sound of loud trumpets and many voices shouting jolts you, and Talmai looks at you with wide-eyed fear. "What was that?"

Before you can answer, the wall of the city begins falling around you. You dodge falling debris, still trying to get to Aunt Rahab's. Her door is in sight. You pull Talmai with you as you work your way in that direction. You hear something above you. Rocks from a crumbling house are falling toward your head!

Talmai pulls you aside. You tumble to the ground, but unbelievably, none of the rocks lands on you. But now you will have to climb a small mountain to get to Aunt Rahab's. You are shocked to realize how silent everything is. Then you hear shouts and screams. Israelite soldiers are attacking and killing anyone left alive. Aunt Rahab's door is only a few feet away. The soldiers are approaching. Can you make it?

"Aunt Rahab! Aunt Rahab!" you shout. The door flies open. Two of your uncles rush out and grab Talmai. You are almost to the door. You trip on loose stones, but your hand lands inside the doorway. Your father's strong arms pull you in and shut the door just in time. Your father, mother, Onan, Talmai, and you are in Aunt Rahab's house.

You give your parents a hug. You and your family are safe!

THE END

You decide not to say anything. You just listen. Aunt Rahab tells the soldiers, "Those men—the ones you say are from Israel—have already left the city. If you hurry, you can catch them."

When the soldiers are gone, Aunt Rahab turns to you. "I'm so happy to see you, dear! But would you mind coming back another time? I have something I need to do."

Your aunt is up to something! You leave, but you sneak up onto the city wall to spy on her house. You watch her door on the inside part of the wall until the moon is bright. The breeze is getting chilly, and you are about to give up and go home when you hear movement on the outside of the wall. You rush over to the edge. A long rope is being let down from Aunt Rahab's window. A shadowy figure slides through her window and climbs down the rope to the ground. Another follows. The second person is halfway down the wall.

CHOICE ONE: If you hold still until the men are out of sight, go to page 29.

CHOICE TWO: If you try to get closer to see better, go to page 42.

You return to the hills and wait for the city gates to open. Israel comes back and marches around the wall every day. One day, they don't stop after the first time around. They keep marching. You try to count how many times they march around Jericho. Is it seven? Suddenly, the trumpets sound louder, and there is a roar of shouting people. All at once, the wall of the city collapses! The Israelites charge in over the crumbled wall. You tremble as you watch your hometown being destroyed. Tears stream down your face. You hold tightly to your sleeping brother.

When you are about to give up hope, you notice that one house is still standing. Could it be Aunt Rahab's? It seems to be in about the right place in the wall. A little while later, you see some people being led out of the city by Israelite soldiers. You could not mistake Uncle Izri's funny walk. It has to be your relatives! You hurry to catch up with them, straining to see if your parents and Talmai are with them.

You call, "Wait up," to some cousins at the back of the group. One of them stops the others. When you catch up, your mother is the first to greet you. She wraps you and Onan in her arms and weeps for joy.

"I thought I had lost all of you," she says. "I thank the God of Israel for saving you both!" The three of you are all that is left of your family.

THE END

You turn right. When you reach Aunt Rahab's house, you do not even stop to knock. You throw the door open and shut it fast behind you.

"What's wrong? You look like the king's army is after you," Aunt Rahab says.

You grab her. "It's Israel's God. You've got to save me. I don't want to die."

Aunt Rahab tries to calm you down. "You don't have to die, remember? I told you that if you are in my house when the battle comes, you will be saved. Haven't you heard about Israel's God and all he has done for Israel? He takes good care of his people."

"But why does he want to destroy Jericho?" you ask.

"I don't know," she says. "But this is an evil city, just like the Amorite cities. I believe that Israel's God is good. I am convinced that he is God in heaven and on earth. That's why I helped the spies when they came to me."

She stops and takes your face in her hands. She looks deeply into your eyes. "I believe that Israel's God is the only real God. He will save us— you, me, and our whole family." You see a look of peace in your aunt's eyes. Suddenly, you are not afraid anymore. She lets go.

Soon you are running again, but this time you are running home. You tell Talmai what Aunt Rahab said, and you keep mentioning it to your parents.

One day, you hear that Israel's army is

approaching. The gates of Jericho are barred shut against them. Talmai and you run to one of your hiding places in the wall to watch. Just in case the attack is coming, you pick a place near Aunt Rahab's house.

At the front of the Israelite army, seven men blow trumpets that look like they're made of ram's horns. Armed soldiers follow. Then you see men carrying a large box on poles. Instead of trying to scale the wall or trying to ram down the gate, they just march in a line around the wall of Jericho. Then they leave.

Talmai and you look at each other and shrug. The next day it is the same. And the next. And the next. Their quiet routine scares you more than an outright attack. All the people of the city are getting jittery. They are like trapped rats in a cage. No one knows what Israel plans to do.

On the seventh day, you are expecting the same thing, but things change. You see the men with the trumpets starting around the wall for a second time. This must be the day!

"Come on!" you say, grabbing Talmai's hand. "We've got to go to Aunt Rahab's house now." You hope the rest of your family will come.

When you arrive, you say to your aunt, "Tell Talmai about Israel's powerful God." While she is explaining, the Israelites keep marching. More and more of your relatives are piling into Aunt Rahab's small house. There is no sign of your parents and your little brother, Onan.

You go back to the window to see what is happening. The large box is passing under you. Suddenly, you feel the need to pray to this God of Israel. You ask him to save your family.

Just as the men of Israel begin to give a loud shout, Aunt Rahab's door creaks open. Your parents walk through it. When your mother sets Onan down, he runs toward you and Talmai. You pick Onan up and hug him, giving thanks to Israel's God for saving your family.

THE END

On the fifth day, you try another tactic to get your father to Aunt Rahab's house. You wake up early and gather your father's cloak, girdle, and sandals. His tunic will look funny without the girdle around his waist, and that will embarrass him. Besides, he needs the girdle to hold his knife and other tools. Talmai sees what you are doing, but he does not give you away. You sneak out of the house and go to Aunt Rahab's early.

Just as you planned, your father comes to Aunt Rahab's with your mother and brothers to retrieve his clothes.

"Since you're here," Aunt Rahab says, "You might as well break the fast with us." Your father stays to eat, but he leaves before the Israelites starts marching around Jericho. You are disappointed that your tactic failed.

The next morning, you take your father's clothes and his money. Without his money, he can't give change to his customers. Again, he comes to Aunt Rahab's house to get his things.

"Please stay with us," you say.

"Not today," your father says with a grimace. He stays to eat the morning meal and talks for a while with other relatives. When the Israelites have marched halfway around the city, he leaves just in case he has customers.

On the seventh day, you take his clothes, his money, his knife, and his ledger. He can't possibly do business without those things. He comes to Aunt Rahab's and walks in laughing.

"You've convinced me. I'll stay. Business is bad anyway. The people seem to prefer watching the Israelites marching more than eating my food."

You all watch out the window. Today is different. Instead of going around once, the army marches around Jericho many times. Talmai counts seven. Suddenly, they all stop. The trumpets sound, clear and loud.

Then you hear a deafening roar of voices and rumblings like the earth is quaking. You all huddle in the middle of the room. You close your eyes until the noise dies down. When you open them, you can see clouds of dust, but nothing in Aunt Rahab's house has been broken except a clay pot.

You hold your breath. The world seems to be moving fast and slowly at the same time. By the time the door opens and Israelite soldiers enter, you are not quite sure what is happening. The soldiers lead your family through Jericho. You see that the wall has fallen, and Israelite soldiers are killing everyone in the city.

You feel panicky until your father says, "You saved my life." Then slowly, your world rights itself. You and your family are safe. Your father slides his arm around your shoulders, and you leave Jericho together under the protection of Israel's God.

THE END

You feel like running as far away as you can, but you think of baby Onan and your parents. "Let's go back home and tell Mom and Dad what we saw," you say. "Maybe if we all go to Aunt Rahab's, Israel's God won't destroy us."

Talmai looks doubtful, but he is too scared to argue with you. You start for home.

When you arrive in Jericho, the city seems the same as when you left it. If only the people knew what you had just seen! You race home, but no one is there.

"Let's check the inn," Talmai says.

You find your parents there. Your mother is helping serve food to guests. The lamb and lentil dish that your mother is serving smells good. Your stomach growls. Onan is playing peacefully behind a chair.

"Where have you two been?" your mother asks. "I've been so worried about you!"

"To the Jordan River to see the Israelite Camp," you say.

Talmai interrupts, "They made the river stop! Just like that!" He claps his hands for emphasis. Everyone in the inn starts to chuckle. You can see that no one believes Talmai.

You rise to his defense. "It's true. We saw it! They carried a big gold box into the water and suddenly they were walking on dry ground. They didn't even get their feet muddy." This time, only some laugh.

"Your children have had too much sun," one man says to your father. He slaps his hand on the table for emphasis and stands up to leave. Others look at you strangely as if they are wondering if your story could be true.

"Enough of this nonsense," your father says. You can tell he is embarrassed. "Take your baby brother home and get to your chores, both of you."

That evening you try again to convince your parents about what you saw. Talmai and you repeat your story. Your parents think it is just another of your wild, made-up spy tales.

Your father concludes, "This time you even scared yourself." He laughs. You feel your face turning red. What can you do to make your mother and him understand?

CHOICE ONE: If you calm yourself down and try to tell your story again, go to page 45.

CHOICE TWO: If you start yelling and waving your arms trying to convince them, go to page 24.

Each day, you ask Aunt Rahab, "Do you think my family will come today?" She shakes her head no. You look out her window, past the scarlet cord she has hung as a signal to Israel. Israel has crossed the Jordan River and is now camped on the plains.

You could go and beg your family to come to Aunt Rahab's, but what if Israel attacks while you are away? You might not be able to make it back in time. You can never quite bring yourself to leave the house. One day the door opens to reveal an older man.

"Grandfather!" you say and give him a big hug. Another day, the door opens and Uncle Ui is there with his wife and three daughters. Aunt Rahab's house is becoming crowded, but at least there are other children to play with.

Aunt Rahab feeds you well, but you miss the herbs that your mother used. The lamb your mother cooked seemed to melt in your mouth. Every day, a few more relatives join you at Aunt Rahab's. She has done a good job of convincing everyone—except your family.

When the attack comes, you are saved, along with many other relatives. You try not to think about your family. You know they are dead, but the idea hurts too much. For the rest of your life, you regret that you were not bold enough to leave Aunt Rahab's house to try to save your family.

THE END

You turn left. The city gates loom up in front of you. They are open. You do not even stop to look back. You feel tingling on your spine as though someone or something is following you, so you run faster. Your mind dulls your senses in a nightmare of terror. You keep running. Finally, you reach a nearby city. You stay there a while, until you hear that Israel's army has defeated Jericho and is on the way.

Then you run again—to the next city, and the next, until finally you can run no more. Your muscles ache, but your mind aches more. You live in the open. No one gives you shelter. A fever makes your eyes hurt when you open them. You know you smell like vomit. You climb to the wall that surrounds the city you now live in. You do not even remember its name. You stand up to breathe some fresh air. In the distance, you see a dust cloud.

"They're coming," someone shouts. "Israel is coming!"

People are screaming and crying all around you. Soldiers are getting ready to fight. You know it is no use. They can't hide from Israel's God. You tried, and it did not work. The thought comes to you that you should have believed Aunt Rahab. You lie back down on the cold stone and prepare to meet your doom.

THE END

You shake your head. "You're believing a lie, Aunt Rahab. They only told you that to make you do what they wanted you to do." With that, you leave.

The next morning, you go to report Aunt Rahab to the king's men. When you get to the palace, one of the guards is yelling at a dog to chase it away. The dog obviously wants food. It sits down in front of the man, turns its head sideways, and whines.

Finally, the guard kicks the poor dog and yells, "Get away from here!" It leaves.

You hesitate. What if the guard kicks you, too? You start to turn away and go home. Then you remember that your city is in danger because of your aunt. You walk up to the guard. He scowls at you.

"What do you want?" he says as though you are the most disgusting person alive.

"I … I want to report some spies," you say.

"Get out of here!" He yells. "You're a day late." He turns his back, refusing even to look at you again.

"But I have new information," you say.

The man ignores you. He walks away. You try another guard. He pushes you away. You fall backwards onto the ground. The soldiers all laugh. No one will listen to your information. You give up and go home.

When you get home, you find Aunt Rahab talking with your mother. After Aunt Rahab leaves, you tell the whole family what you saw. You tell them not to believe anything Aunt Rahab says, because she is a traitor.

From then on, you and your brother Talmai practice every day with swords. You pretend you are fighting Israel. Of course, in your games Jericho always wins.

Finally, the attack comes. The wall of Jericho has fallen, and Talmai and you stand side-by-side to meet the enemy. Two Israelites are coming toward you. Your sword meets one man's with a clank. His strength surprises you. With all your might, you try to hold him off. Suddenly, Talmai falls against your leg.

"No!" you scream. You feel steel plunging into your own stomach. You both die fighting.

THE END

You decide that you can't stand feeling trapped. Your mother will eventually make up with her sister. Meanwhile, you can find out what is going on and report to everyone.

You visit Aunt Rahab every day and spend most of your time staring out the window. You rest your elbow on the windowsill and feel something uncomfortable under it. A red cord is hanging from the window.

"What's this doing here," you ask, starting to remove it.

Aunt Rahab panics. "No! Don't touch that! That red cord is the only way the Israelites will know where to find us." You are beginning to understand how deeply Aunt Rahab believes that she will be saved.

Soon the Israelites come into view, but not to attack. They seem to be using Jericho only for marching and music practice. You think it is funny. Lots of people in Jericho are watching from windows in the wall. After six days of this, you tell your family that Aunt Rahab's window has the best view of the parade.

"I miss my sister." Your mother shrugs. "I'll go with you tomorrow."

Your father nods. "I've heard so much about these parades but haven't seen one yet. You say Aunt Rahab has a good view from her window?"

"The best," you say.

"Then I'll go, too," your father says. "We're

not doing much business at the inn now anyway. Talmai and Onan can also go."

The next day, you are all watching from the window.

"It's an odd march," your father says. "The trumpets play, but the people are silent. They don't even sound a war cry."

"Except for those horns," your mother says. She covers her ears. Other relatives are with you. Most of them are nervous because they believe Israel is about to attack. Aunt Rahab tries to calm them with dates and fresh bread. Your fingers grow sticky.

Suddenly, the Israelites stop and look up. One is looking straight at you. They shout and the trumpets blare. A chill runs through you. Everything turns to chaos—grating noises, shaking walls, screaming villagers. You fall to the floor.

When it is over, you look out the window again. All around Aunt Rahab's house, the wall has fallen. You check to make sure the red cord is still attached. After you are rescued and taken to the Israelite camp, all of your family wants to know about Israel's God.

THE END

You and your relatives are certain that the attack will be today … at any moment. You are afraid that your family will not get to Aunt Rahab's in time. You ask your aunt to watch Onan, and you rush out the door.

You bump into people as you race through the streets, but you keep running.

"Are they marching again?" a voice asks.

"Of course they are," says another. "Every day it's the same silly religious parade." No one laughs. You can tell that Israel's marching is wearing on their nerves.

When you reach home, no one is there. Maybe they went to Aunt Rahab's, and you missed them on the way. You have a nagging feeling that you are wrong. Is there time to go to the inn? You must take that chance.

Your lungs feel like they are going to burst as you fly through the inn's door. Your parents and Talmai are inside.

"Please come now!" you shout between breaths. "I've been watching the Israelites. The attack is coming, and there will be no escape! Only Aunt Rahab's house is safe!"

Your parents believe you, but your brother hesitates. You grab your brother's arm and try to drag him with you.

He pulls away. "Why shouldn't we stand and fight for our city?" he asks.

You have only one answer, and you know it is the right one, thanks to Aunt Rahab. "Because their God is God."

Talmai's eyes change from stubbornness, to wonder, and then instantly to fear. He grabs your hand, and you all run for Aunt Rahab's house. Just as you turn the corner onto her street, the ground begins to shake. The wall of the city is crumbling before your eyes. The door is almost within reach. You trip. Talmai picks you up, and you make it through the door just in time.

THE END

"I can't believe that you lied to the king's men," you tell Aunt Rahab. "Those spies are still here, aren't they?" You lower your voice. "Did they threaten you? I can run after the soldiers and bring them back."

"No, we don't need the soldiers. I know what I'm doing. Israel's God is powerful—not like Jericho's gods," she says. "He has helped Israel defeat mighty enemies."

You cannot believe what you are hearing. Is Aunt Rahab actually on Israel's side? You grab a grape from her table. Eating always helps you think. It is sour, though, so you grab some plumper, sweeter ones to cover the taste.

"Jericho is strong," you say. The Israelites can't possibly get through our wall." You kick your foot against the wooden chair.

"I believe their God can help them do anything. If they attack our city, they will win."

You want to think more about this, but your stomach is calling for food. "I have to go home for supper." You promise not to say anything to anyone.

During supper you are quiet. You look at each of your family members—strong Talmai, sweet Onan, your beautiful mother, and your caring father—and wonder what will happen to them if Israel attacks. After supper you rush back to Aunt Rahab's.

"Are they still here?" you whisper when she answers the door.

"No," Aunt Rahab says.

You breathe easier. "Tell me more about this God of Israel."

"Walls, seas, and powerful armies are no match for this God. Jericho will fall, but don't worry. Anyone who is in my house when the attack comes will be safe."

Your head is spinning. Finally you come to a decision. "I don't know why," you say, "but I believe that what you say is true." You help her tie a red cord in her window.

"This cord is a sign for Israel's army. It is a secret signal to let them know that I live here. When the attack comes, they will see this cord and come to rescue me and any of my father's house who is here."

"So the cord is there to help protect you?" you ask.

"Yes," Aunt Rahab says. "It will protect my house from destruction."

"Then we have to make sure that the cord doesn't come loose," you say.

"That can be your job. Will you keep check-ing it for me?"

You agree to go to Aunt Rahab's house every day to check the cord. When the attack comes, you are safe.

THE END

On the fifth day, you go to the inn with your father. "If you choose to die, then I'll die with you," you say. You hope he will go to Aunt Rahab's for your sake if not for his. You cook, clean, and serve meals with him.

"I saw the parade yesterday," says a customer. Others laugh as he continues, "Even my three-legged dog could beat that sorry excuse for an army."

Another customer adds, "Those cowards just walk around their enemies. Someone should tell them that it's the fighting and not the walking that wins wars." More laughter.

The first man says, "Cowards is the right name for them." Others laugh, but they keep looking out the windows as if they are expecting to see Israel at any time. You sweep the floor at the end of the day and hope that your father will go to Aunt Rahab's with you the next morning.

Your father is determined to stay open for business but makes you go to Aunt Rahab's the next day with the family. You leave for Aunt Rahab's with the others. Once there, you begin to grow bored. You wonder if the Israelites plan to attack at all. On the seventh day, you help your father at the inn again. Business is really slow.

You are stirring food over the fire when a friend hurries in and says, "The Israelites are doing something different today. Their parade isn't going around just once. They're already on their fifth rotation." The change in the marching pattern frightens you.

"Go with me to Aunt Rahab's," you beg your father.

"We might as well," your father says. Just then a customer comes into the inn and orders a leg of lamb. Your father smiles. He tells you, "Let me finish this order, and then we'll go."

"Hurry! Please hurry," you say. You go to the window and look out to the street. "Can we go now? Are you almost done?"

"A few more minutes," your father says.

The man is a slow eater. As your father sets a bowl of water on the table for the man to clean his hands, you hear people yelling. Then the floor begins to jiggle. Soon the earth is shaking. A deafening roar follows. You run to your father and grab his arm. The roof of the inn collapses over your heads and kills your father, his customer, and you.

THE END

You do not believe the rumors. All Israel has done for the past six days is march around and blow horns. They are just noisemakers. You are laughing about it when you hear frantic knocking at the door. It is your cousins.

They pull on your arm. "Come with us to Aunt Rahab's house now. Otherwise, you will die." Onan is playing on the floor nearby. On impulse, you grab him and run. You call to the rest of your family, but no one else follows. You have just made it into Aunt Rahab's house when the wall of the city comes crashing down.

"How did they destroy Jericho's wall?" you ask no one in particular.

Standing at the window, your Uncle Ui says, "I don't know. I saw the whole thing, but Israel never even touched the wall. It had to be their God who destroyed it."

Maybe Israel's God is as great as people were saying! Soon Israelite soldiers come through the door and lead you to safety. You never see the rest of your family again, but you and Onan live with Aunt Rahab, and you follow the God of Israel for the rest of your lives.

THE END

After your parents leave the table, you tell Talmai, "I'll tell you everything, but first I have to fix my sandal while the light is good." Talmai helps you get the tools you need. You sit together outside the house as you work.

"You should have seen the spies today," you begin. His face brightens. You continue, "They were dressed in tan tunics with brown cloaks. I thought it was far too warm for the cloaks. That's what made me suspect them at once. They had their heads covered, but I could see that one of them had curly hair."

"How did you know they were Israelites?"

"I heard two men talking about them. They said something about their powerful God drowning the whole Egyptian army." You place a leather strap in your mouth to stretch it. When the strap looks right, you spit it out and get a drink of water to rinse out the leather taste. You say, "I think they were exaggerating, don't you?"

He nods. "But what about Aunt Rahab? Is she really in danger?"

"She might be." You look up to make sure your parents are not around and lower your voice. "The spies went into her house."

Just then your father walks up the street toward you. "What are you two troublemakers doing?"

Instead of answering, you say, "I already fed

the livestock." He nods. You both follow him inside. The lamb from earlier has been cut up and is cooking over the fire into some type of soup for tomorrow. You like it when your house smells like this.

"Israelite spies were seen in the city today," your father says to no one in particular, "but they've gone. The king's men are giving chase."

"I wish I could have gone with the king's men," says Talmai.

"I would have liked to watch the chase from the top of the wall," you add.

"You have enough to do helping out around here," says your father. "Which reminds me. I need both of you to work at the inn tomorrow before we open for business." You groan.

The next morning, you have just returned from the inn when Aunt Rahab comes to visit. Before she can tell you hello, Talmai asks in a loud voice, "What was it like to have spies in your house?" She seems surprised that you know about her visitors.

"Is it true that their God opened the sea and killed the whole Egyptian army?" you ask. "Our gods have never done anything like that."

"That's because our gods are made by people," Aunt Rahab says. "They're just made out of metal, wood, or rocks—just like the ones that you kick around. They have no power. But Israel's God is alive! I believe he is the only true God."

Your mother drops the bowl of beans she is preparing. The bowl does not crack, but beans are everywhere. You are glad your father is at the inn. He would not like this kind of talk. You all help your mother gather the spilled beans.

Onan grabs a handful and toddles away with them, giggling. You chase him and take the beans from his hands. You give him two rocks to play with and set him on your lap. You stick a bean in your mouth and enjoy its fresh, crunchy flavor.

Aunt Rahab now directs her words to your mother. "Shebna, you have to believe me. Israel's God will destroy Jericho. Everyone who is not inside my house during the battle will be killed. Promise that you will come to my house."

Your mother's eyebrows draw together. "I'll think about it, Rahab, but I won't promise. I must talk this over with my husband." Aunt Rahab smiles and leaves.

CHOICE ONE: If you do not believe what Aunt Rahab says, go to page 38.

CHOICE TWO: If believe what Aunt Rahab says, go to page 13.

Trapped!

Spiritual Building Block: **Worship**

You can do the following things to give honor to the one and only God:

Think About It:

We do not worship gods of stone and wood, but we sometimes put things before God: money, friends, self. Ask God to help you think about what you value more than God. Ask God to forgive you for having another "god;" also ask him to fill you with his Spirit so that you can honor only him.

Talk About It:

Be bold about your faith in the one true God. Make decisions based on who you are in Christ and then talk about it with others. This will increase your faith, build up others, and honor God. When you struggle with your faith, talk about that, too. God blesses the person of integrity.

Try It:

Don't just ask God for things. Spend time worshipping him, too. Tell him what you love about him. Thank him. God is so good: there is no darkness in him at all! Once you get started in praising him for that, you won't want to quit.

COLLECT THEM ALL!

DEADLY EXPEDITION!

Imagine that your decisions determine whether you will ever enter the Promised Land.

You and your entire nation of Hebrew slaves have just escaped from the Egyptians and are heading toward the land that God has promised to give you. But when you reach the Red Sea, you look behind to see the entire Egyptian army closing in on you! You must make a choice. Will you stand and fight the Egyptian army? Or will you trust God and miraculously cross the sea on a dry path—only to face the possibility of battling yet another nation? You must make a choice.

ESCAPE!

Imagine that your decisions have the power to determine the fate of many Christians.

You have become a believer of Jesus Christ—even though you know you might die because of it. You see one of your favorite Christians, Stephen, being dragged off by temple officials to be killed for his faith. You must make a choice. You run off to warn your family that danger is coming. As you are leaving, you overhear people making plans to raid the home of your good friends. You must make a choice.

ATTACK!

Imagine that your decisions have the power to determine the fate of your country.

One day, while you are guarding your family's sheep, a bully attacks you from behind and steals your prized possession. You must make a choice. You abandon the sheep and chase the bully and almost catch him when you both see a huge foreign army in the distance. You must make a choice. Do you forget the differences you have with the bully, or work together to see what the foreigners are up to? You must make a choice.